FOREWORD

After what I call my "dirty little intermission" (the uncensored *Left Field RAW* editions), I've returned to the conventional format with fresh material.
In parallel with the book's theme, I've braved some "choppy waters" myself as far as major changes in my personal life. I also had the joy of testing those waters by attending three different bookselling/signing events in the past year. The positive feedback from others has been truly gratifying.
As it always has, it's been a good experience challenging myself with new cartoon material as well as new design concepts.
And as the title implies, this is truly a "return" book, coming full circle like a shark fin to re-connect with the earlier books.
So it's my pleasure to say to my readers: WELCOME BACK TO *LEFT FIELD*!
And of course: enjoy the book!

Yours truly,

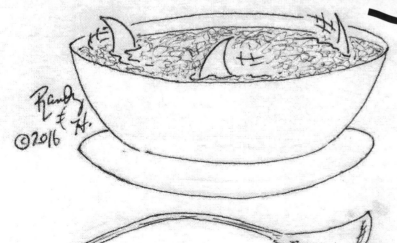

JUST WHEN YOU THOUGHT IT WAS SAFE...

LEFT ★ FIELD RETURNS ™

more biting cartoon humor

Randy Halford

AuthorHouse™
1663 Liberty Drive
Bloomington, IN 47403
www.authorhouse.com
Phone: 1 (800) 839-8640

Published by AuthorHouse 06/08/2016

ISBN: 978-1-5246-1252-8 (sc)
ISBN: 978-1-5246-1251-1 (e)

Print information available on the last page.

Any people depicted in stock imagery provided by Thinkstock are models,
and such images are being used for illustrative purposes only.
Certain stock imagery © Thinkstock.

This book is printed on acid-free paper.

NARCOLEPTIC KINDERGARTEN

FROG TELEVISION

EXECUTING COMEDY

THE FLASH LEAVES A NOTE

SNOW WHITE'S EIGHTH DWARF THAT JUST HAD TO GO:
HECKLEY...

9

Tea and Crumpet CINEMA

now playing:
"GRUMPY OLD CHAPS"

coming soon:

"GOODBYE, MR. FISH 'N CHIPS"
THE "BIG BEN LEBOWSKI"
"THREE BLOKES AND A BABY"
"PULP PUB FICTION"
"FOG DAY AFTERNOON"
"DOUBLE DECKER BUS JEOPARDY"
"JURASSIC PARLIAMENT"
THE "LONGEST SCOTLAND YARD"
"PICCADILLY CIRCUS OF THE CARIBBEAN"
"U.K. MARSHALS"
"SEARCHING FOR BOBBIES FISCHER"
"THOUSANDS CHEERIO"
THE "WILD WILD WESTMINSTER ABBEY"
THE "LONDON BRIDGES OF MADISON COUNTY"
"CASINO ROYALE FAMILY"

Banks H. ©2012

BRITISH FLICKS

JUST SEEING IF YOU'RE PAYING ATTENTION.

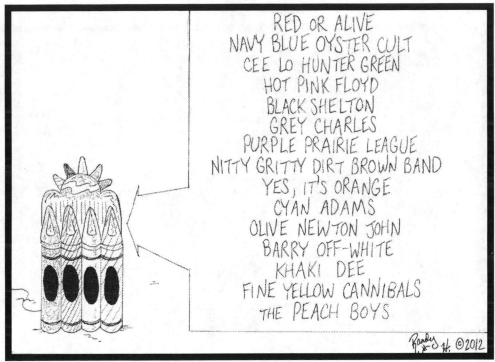

CRAYON JUKEBOXES

"YOU MISUNDERSTOOD ME! WHAT I MEANT WAS, I'D SELL MY SALE TO GET MORE BUSINESS IN HERE!"

THE NATURE FILM "MOLASSES MALLARD; WORLD'S LAZIEST DUCK"

15

CENTIPEDE SELF-HELP VIDEOS

TRIVIAL FORTUNE TELLERS

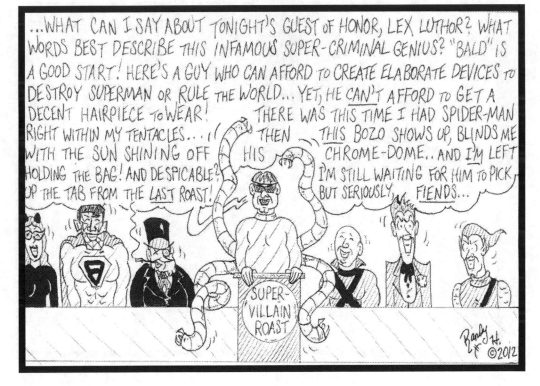

21

WHEN ERIC CLAPTON SANG "I SHOT THE SHERIFF, BUT I DID NOT SHOOT THE DEPUTY"...

DID IT MEAN HE FAVORED THE DEPUTY?!

©2012

DEEP THOUGHTS GRAFFITI

"SOUTH PACIFIER"

"A STREETCAR NAMED DIAPERS"

"CRIBARET"

"SUGAR-TEETHING BABIES"

"HOW TO SUCCEED IN BABY TALK WITHOUT REALLY TRYING"

"THE PRODUCERS OF FORMULA"

BABY BROADWAY

23

24

"WELL, HERE WE GO AGAIN, JOE! ANOTHER LONG DAY OF BUSTING OUR HUMPS... AND GETTING PAID WORTH SPIT!"

FISH TELEVISION

SHRINK RAP

Wantannodalooki FLIX

now playing:

"300 PINEAPPLES"

coming soon:

"MY LUAU WITH ANDRE"
"HONOLULU, I SHRUNK THE KIDS"
"SPLENDOR IN THE GRASS SKIRT"
"LEI MISERABLES"
"THE SUGARCANELAND EXPRESS"
"LAVA STORY"
"TORCH DANCES WITH WOLVES"
"THE POI WHO COULD FLY"
"YOURS, MAUI AND OURS"
"HULA FRAMED ROGER RABBIT"
"THE PALM TREES BEACH STORY"
"BLUE WATER FOR ELEPHANTS"
"NATIONAL LAMPOON'S CRABBY VACATION"
"TITANIC TIKI BARS"

Randy H. ©201

GOING HAWAIIAN AT THE MOVIES

GYM BUNNIES

30

NATIONWIDE BUDGET IN THE RED; PRESIDENT TURNING BLACK & BLUE FROM PURPLE-FACED CRITICS WHO DECLARE WHITE HOUSE STAFF IS "YELLOW"	PRINCE CAUGHT IN UPRIGHT WASHING MACHINE; GETS ROYALLY AGITATED	GIRL SCOUT TROOP FOOD POISONED, LOSES COOKIES
"YADA YADA" BECOMES NEW "WHATEVER"	MAN THINKS OUTSIDE BOX; FALLS TO DEATH OUTSIDE APARTMENT BUILDING	PERSON SHOT, STABBED AND BEATEN MANAGES TO FINISH "WAR AND PEACE"

©2012

OUTRAGEOUS HEADLINES

TOOL INJURIES

DEEP THOUGHTS GRAFFITI, PART 2

UNKNOWN MOMENTS IN MUSIC HISTORY

T.V.'s "THE REAL SCARECROW AND MRS. KING"

STINK BUG RELATIONSHIPS

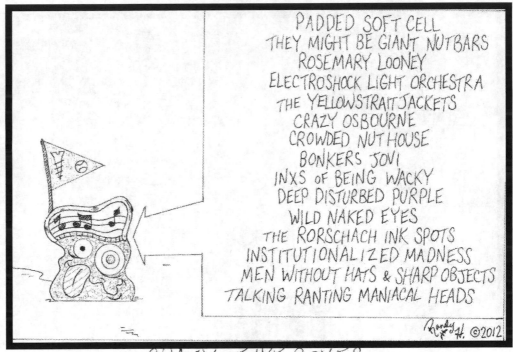

CRAZY JUKE BOXES

37

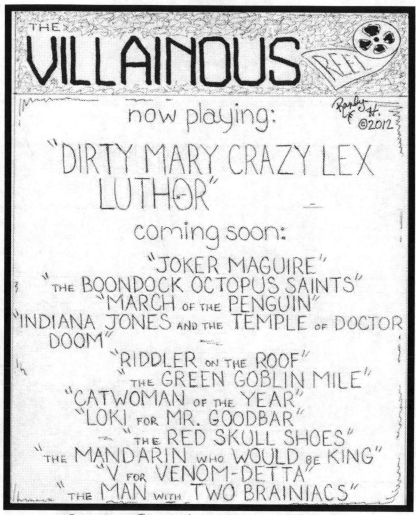

THE

VILLAINOUS REEL

now playing:

"DIRTY MARY CRAZY LEX LUTHOR"

coming soon:

"JOKER MAGUIRE"
"THE BOONDOCK OCTOPUS SAINTS"
"MARCH OF THE PENGUIN"
"INDIANA JONES AND THE TEMPLE OF DOCTOR DOOM"
"RIDDLER ON THE ROOF"
"THE GREEN GOBLIN MILE"
"CATWOMAN OF THE YEAR"
"LOKI FOR MR. GOODBAR"
"THE RED SKULL SHOES"
"THE MANDARIN WHO WOULD BE KING"
"V FOR VENOM-DETTA"
"THE MAN WITH TWO BRAINIACS"

SUPER-EVIL CELLULOID

OPTOMETRY FOR THE LAZY EYE

I LOVE LOOSE MEAT SANDW. | HOAGIE'S HEROES
MAGNUM, PBJ | HOW I MEATBALL YOUR MOTHER
MARY TUNA MOORE | THIS OLD DELI | LAW & ORDER: BLTE
BOLOGNA BONANZA | ROAST BEEF-WITCHED | NEW
EXTRA MAYO | LAVERNE & TURKEY | DIAGNOSIS MUSTARD
WRYE IN CINCINNATI | LOST BAGS of CHIPS | MOVI
THE SALAMI SIMPSONS | PASTRAMI LEWIS CAN'T LOSE
THE JERSEY SHORE with CHEESE | THE BIG SUB THEORY

SANDWICH TELEVISION

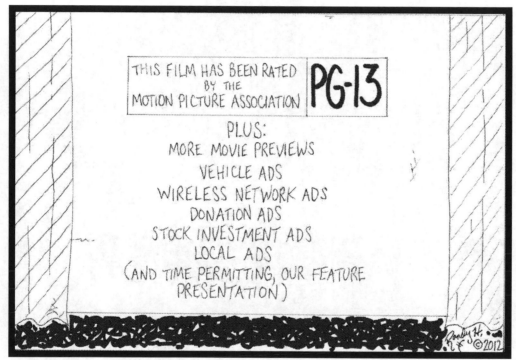

THIS FILM HAS BEEN RATED BY THE MOTION PICTURE ASSOCIATION — PG-13
PLUS:
MORE MOVIE PREVIEWS
VEHICLE ADS
WIRELESS NETWORK ADS
DONATION ADS
STOCK INVESTMENT ADS
LOCAL ADS
(AND TIME PERMITTING, OUR FEATURE PRESENTATION)

THOSE RIDICULOUSLY LONG PRE-MOVIE PROMOS of MODERN TIMES

A TYPICAL DAY AT DEAN'S HOUSE OF BEANS

FIBER ZOMBIES

EXAMPLES of WHEN HOLIDAYS GET DOWNSIZED

45

MORON MOVIES

GYM RATS

WE'VE ONLY JUST BEGUN

TROLL BANTER

DUMB JUNGLE TRICKS

"HAPPY DAYS" TELEVISION

54

RIDING THROUGH WESTERN CLICHE COUNTY

MOUSE TRAP flix

Randy H. © 2013

now playing:

"SNOW WHITE CHRISTMAS"

coming soon:

"THE MICKEY MOUSE THAT ROARED"
"THE DONALD DUCKS OF HAZZARD"
"GOOFY GLADIATOR"
"DUMBO AND DUMBER"
"PINOCCHIO OF THE CARIBBEAN"
"CINDERELLA KANE"
"THE GOOD, THE BAMBI AND THE UGLY"
"NEVER SAY NEVERLAND AGAIN"
"LADY AND THE TRAMP SINGS THE BLUES"
"THE BIG SLEEPING BEAUTY"
"101 DALMATIANS FLEW OVER THE CUCKOO'S NEST"

"FANTASIA FOUR"
"DIRTY MARY POPPINS CRAZY LARRY"
"GEORGE OF THE JUNGLE BOOK"
"LITTLE MERMAID WOMEN"

OTHER FILMS, DISNEY-STYLE

58

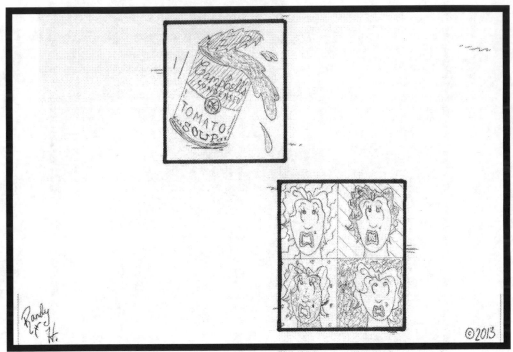

AT THE ANDY WARHOL MUSEUM

MIDDLE-AGED WOOD STOVES

63

© 2013

EDDIE RABBI
LDS ZEPPELIN
BUDDHA HOLLY
THE STEEPLE SINGERS
PULPIT ENEMY
THE ALAN PARSONS PROTESTANT
THE RIGHTEOUSLY FANATIC BROTHERS
SAVIOR McLACHLAN
THE HOLIES
THE PREACH BOYS
BOOK OF GENESIS
LADY MADONNA ANTEBELLUM
STAINED GLASS TIGER
VIRGIN MARY J. BLIGE
JUSTIN BIBLE

OF THEE I SING

RELIGIOUS JUKEBOXES, PART 2

PIG BALLETS

65

PRINT IS DEAD.

ILLITERACY AND ABBREVIATIONS ARE ALIVE AND WELL.

— H.S. DROPOUT

DEEP THOUGHTS GRAFFITI, PART 3

66

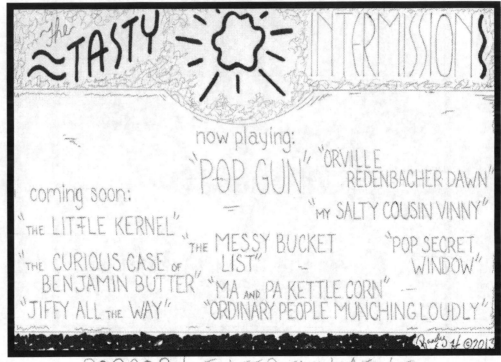

now playing:
"POP GUN" "ORVILLE REDENBACHER DAWN"

coming soon: "MY SALTY COUSIN VINNY"
"THE LITTLE KERNEL"
                        "THE MESSY BUCKET   "POP SECRET
"THE CURIOUS CASE of   LIST"   WINDOW"
   BENJAMIN BUTTER"   "MA AND PA KETTLE CORN"
"JIFFY ALL THE WAY"   "ORDINARY PEOPLE MUNCHING LOUDLY"

POPCORN ENTERTAINMENT

HOLLYWOOD STUNT MONSTERS

68

ROYAL PAINS

"YEAH. SURE. IGNORE ME FOR NOW. BUT EVENTUALLY, YOU'LL HAVE TO ADDRESS THE ELEPHANT IN THE ROOM!"

PLANET TELEVISION

WHY INTERNET-BASED SUPER-HERO PROGRAMS OFTEN FAIL

DONALD TRUMP'S PETS

75

THE POINDEXTER SISTERS
DORKY PARTON
EMINe=mc²
THE GUESS WHO WEARS HIGHWATERS
GEEKI DEE
THE POCKET PROTECTOR PRETENDERS
THEY MIGHT BE GENIUSES
HIGH I.Q. 10,000 MANIACS
NO DOUBT, YOU'RE SMART
THREE DORK NIGHT
NERD HERDER
BJORK SNEEZED THE GUY IN THE THICK GLASSES
NO SIMPLE MINDS
ALICIA KEYS TO THE SCIENCE LAB
RUN-DMCU AT THE TREKKIE CONVENTION

NERDY JUKE BOXES

IF NEW TECHNOLOGY JUNKIES "TEXT"...

AND NAUGHTY PEOPLE "SEXT"...

THEN DO WITCHES "HEXT"?

DEEP THOUGHTS GRAFFITI, PART 4

YEAH BABY theatre

now playing:

"DIAPER HARD"

coming soon:

"RATTLE of the BULGE"
"THE PINK & BLUE PAJAMA GAME"
"PACIFIER HEIGHTS"
"THEY CALL ME MISTER CRIBS!"
"TEETHING MUTANT NINJA TURTLES"
"PLAYSKOOL MISTY FOR ME"
"DIVINE SECRETS of the GOO-GOO GA-GA
SISTERHOOD"
"BEACH NAP-TIME BLANKET BINGO"
"RIDING IN CARRIAGES WITH BOYS"
"TODDLER RECALL"
"THE STRAINED FOOD OF THE GODS"
"WYATT BURP"
"THEY DROOL BY NIGHT"

Ranby Jr. ©2013

INFANT FLICKS

DR. THICKHEAD, THE MOST CLUELESS JAMES BOND VILLAIN, PART 3

THE LEAN FAMILY GOES TO ITALY

82

84

THIS IS WHAT THEY GET FOR NEVER LETTING POOR RUDOLPH JOIN IN ANY REINDEER GAMES...

"ABBOT" & COSTELLO

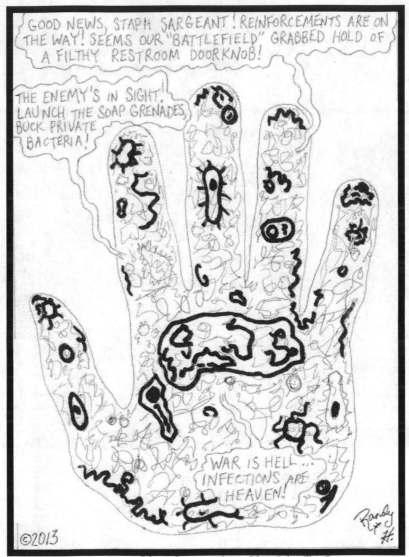

GERM WARFARE

"GOODFELLAS" TELEVISION

HOW TECHNOLOGY CAN "ISOLATE" HUMAN INTERACTION

COSTCO FOR THE OLD

CATS AND DOGS DEALING WITH BOREDOM

Moin' Contraption HOUSE

now playing:

"THE WIZARD of OZARKS"

coming soon:

"MOONSHINE over MIAMI"
"NEXT of KINFOLK"
"FUEDIN' NEMO"
"THE LONGEST BEARDED DAY"
"MY BEST FRIEND'S SHOTGUN WEDDING"
"MOTHER, HOOCH JUGS & SPEED"
"PLAY it AGAIN, BANJO SAM"
"MY POSSUM DINNER with ANDRE"
"GOOD WILL HUNTING DOG"
"BACKWOODS to the FUTURE"
"OLD JALOPY SCHOOL"
"HARRY POTTER and the GOBLET of FIREWATER"
"SPACE JAMBOREE"
"GRANNY TORINO"
"OUTHOUSE of AFRICA"

Randy H ©2013

HILLBILLY PICTURE SHOWS

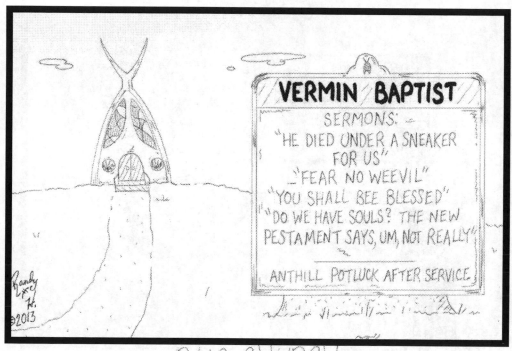

BUG CHURCH

DR. THICKHEAD, THE MOST CLUELESS JAMES BOND VILLAIN, PART 4

95

SONGWRITING COURSES OF THE 90'S

AFTERTHOUGHTS

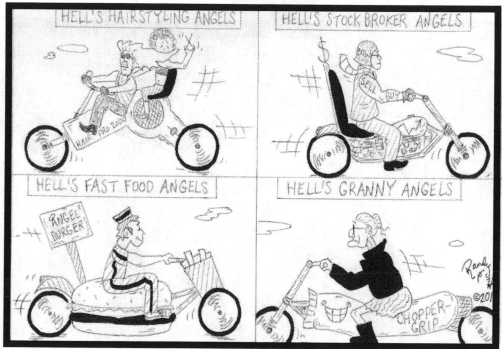

Many Feelings Cinema

now playing:

"ANGRY POWERS:
INTERNATIONAL MADMAN of MYSTERY"

coming soon:

"HAPPY POTTER and the CHAMBER of SMILES"
"MELANCHOLY POPPINS"
"the SAD NEWS BEARS"
"NEVER SAY NERVOUS AGAIN"
"GRUMPY with the WIND"
"JOY STORY"
"MALICE DOESN'T LIVE HERE ANYMORE"
"MISCHIEVOUS CONGENIALITY"
"the TWILIGHT SAGA: BROODING DAWN"
"the MATRIX ELATED"
"WISHY-WASHY UPON a STAR"
"ANXIOUS KARENINA"
"the COMPASSION of the CHRIST"

MOODY MOVIES

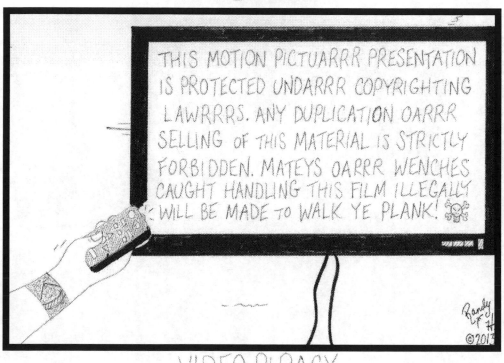

VIDEO PIRACY

Randy F. H. ©2013

SB HOF —
"SMOKING BAMBOO, HUT ON FIRE."

VWTMINBN —
"VILLAGE WITCH TURNED ME INTO NEWT;
   BETTER NOW."

SCLAO! —
"SNAKE CHARMER LAUGHING ASP OFF!"

P4U —
"PESTILENCE FOR YOU."

CTBSDF —
"CAN'T TALK; BUSY SWEEPING DIRT FLOOR."

I ♡ VI —
"I LOVE VILLAGE IDIOCY."

MU@STN2DC —
"MEET YOU AT SPIRIT TOTEM NEXT TO DONKEY
   CART."

MSET2O —
"MY SHADOW EVIL, TRYING TO OUTRUN."

SMALL VILLAGE TEXTING

CHEESY TELEVISION

SPAGHETTI WESTERNS

LOCUST "SPOILER" NOVELS

108

now playing:
"SOFA'S CHOICE"

coming soon:

"ARMOIRE of DARKNESS"
"SEEKING a FRIEND for the END TABLE of the WORLD"
"MY COUCH VINNY"
"KITCHEN DINER"
"COFFEE TABLE and CIGARETTES"
"EASY CHAIR RIDER"
"X-MEN: THE LAST LAMP STAND"
"STARSKY & ENTERTAINMENT HUTCH"
"RETURN of the KING BED"
"THE GOLDEN VANITY of SINBAD"
"NIGHTSTAND at the MUSEUM"
"SHIP of STOOLS"
"ARMCHAIR-AGEDDON"
"DRESSER UNCHAINED"
"THE BOOKCASE of ELI"

FURNISHED ENTERTAINMENT

HITLER'S POOL

CLASSIFIEDS

VOL. 336, ISSUE 110

TUES, MARCH 26, 2013

JOBS

WIFE'S MEATLOAF 2
TOUGH'; HIRE SHARP
KNIFE WHO CAN REALLY
CUT IT —

JOBS 4 UTENSILS. MUCH
TRAVEL /OPPORTUNITIES;
CO. LOOKING 2 STICK FORK
IN ROAD —

CORKSCREW NEEDED 4
WINE PARTY; BIG $ PER
POP —

DATING

KITCHEN ROMANTIC'; FOXY
LADLE ENJOYS SPOONING

PROFESSIONAL MASHER';
POTATO MASHER SEEKS
2 GET DOWN W/SERVING
BOWL

EGG BEATER CAN WHIP
IT GOOD W/ RIGHT MATE

FOR SALE

SPATULA LOOKING 4
NEW HOME, HARD
WORKER; KNOWS HOW
2 GET UNDER SURFACE
OF THINGS —

PEELER KNOWS HOW 2
SHAVE AWAY TIME IN
KITCHEN

NEW WALNUT SHELLER
CRACKS MARKET —

©2013

UTENSIL WANT ADS

111

LEMON "JUMPERS"

"WHO ARE YOU?!"

1 YR, B4C: A & E ☾ G. HR! —
"1 YEAR, BEFORE CLOTHES: ADAM & EVE MOON
    GOD. HOW RUDE!"

SA! N #1 B 2 P W/A —
"SPOILER ALERT! NOAH #1 BOATER TO PARTY
    WITH ANIMALS."

3 WM FBB @ JC BB —
"THREE WISE MEN FLASH BLING-BLING AT J.C.
    BIRTH BASH."

R U G 2 MOS RSP T 2 —
"ARE YOU GOING TO MOSES' RED SEA PARTING
    THING?"

N/A... W 10 C —
"NOT AVAILABLE...WATCHING 'TEN COMMAND-
    MENTS.'"

CDS↑CA; SB A W/H —
"CAIN DOES STAND-UP COMEDY ACT; SLAYS
    BROTHER ABEL WITH HUMOR."

2 CRUC 2-D; G ++'D —
"TWO CRUCIFIED TODAY; GOT DOUBLE-CROSSED."

©2013   Randy F D 7H

EARLY BIBLICAL TEXTING

UN- CINEMA Shelled

now playing:

"WALNUT STREET"

coming soon:

"BEECH BLANKET BINGO"
"CHILDREN of the ACORN"
"TANGO & CASHEW"
"10 THINGS I HAZELNUT ABOUT YOU"
"THE CHESTNUTTY PROFESSOR"
"PECANNERY ROW"
"BACHELOR PARTY SNACK"
"PISTACHIOS of the CARIBBEAN"
"THE TRAIL of the LONESOME PINE NUT"
"HARRY POTTER AND THE GOBLET of FIRE
ROASTED PEANUTS"
"MACADAMIA MAX BEYOND THUNDERDOME"
"ALMOND ABOUT EVE"
"THE MATRIX RESHELLED"

Randy H. ©2013

MOVIES GONE NUTS

WHEN THE ARMY LOSES THEIR WAY

PRIMITIVE VERSIONS of T.V. GAMESHOWS

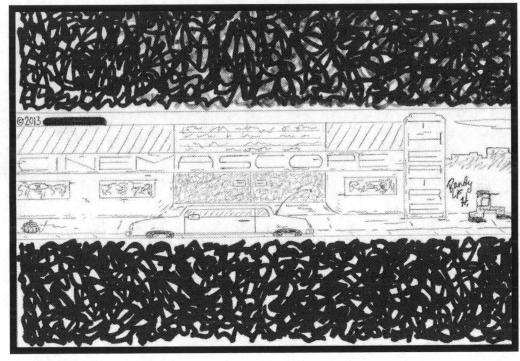

THE RETAIL WESTERN "THEY HAD PRICES ON THEIR HEADS"

123

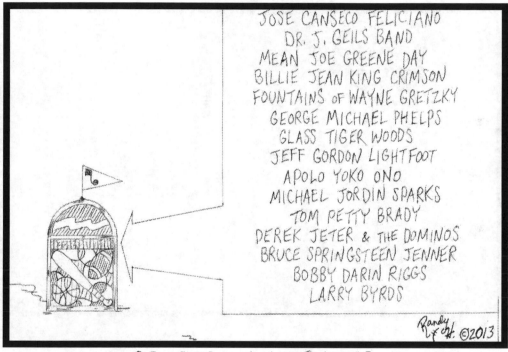

JOSE CANSECO FELICIANO
DR. J. GEILS BAND
MEAN JOE GREENE DAY
BILLIE JEAN KING CRIMSON
FOUNTAINS of WAYNE GRETZKY
GEORGE MICHAEL PHELPS
GLASS TIGER WOODS
JEFF GORDON LIGHTFOOT
APOLO YOKO ONO
MICHAEL JORDIN SPARKS
TOM PETTY BRADY
DEREK JETER & THE DOMINOS
BRUCE SPRINGSTEEN JENNER
BOBBY DARIN RIGGS
LARRY BYRDS

Randy Ft. ©2013

SPORTS JUKEBOXES

"SORRY. BUT WE'RE NOT STICKING OUR NECKS OUT FOR THIS 'THANKSGIVING' THING UNTIL WE TALK TO OUR LAWYER..."

SECRET POLICE

THE WORD "OBSOLETE" DEEMED OBSOLETE	PUNCTUATION MARK HOSPITALIZED; LIES COMMA-TOSE	OPTOMETRIST FOOLS PUBLIC INTO READING THIS HEADLINE
NEARSIGHTED WIFE LASHES OUT IN ANGER; ACCIDENTALLY BROWBEATS HUSBAND	A DEAR MAN RESCUES DEER WHILE RIDING JOHN DEERE	TRENDSETTING DISMISSED AS PEOPLE JUST SHOWING OFF

Randy F. H.
©2013

OUTRAGEOUS HEADLINES, PART 2

"WOW! THIS IS UNEXPECTED! I'M ALL CHOKED UP... I HAVE A HUMAN IN MY THROAT...!"

 "YOU WORE <u>THAT</u>?"

"I HAVE THIS LIP FUNGUS..."

"WHEW! JUST WENT TO THE BATHROOM. NOW I'M READY FOR LUNCH!"

"I SURE MISS MY EX."

"MY DOG LIKES LICKING ALL MY DATES' FACES."

"SO... IS THIS GETTING SOMEWHERE SOON?"

"MY ROOMMATE AND I TAKE SHOWERS TOGETHER."

"CAN MY MOM COME <u>WITH</u> US?"

"I LOST MY JOB. CAN YOU PAY THIS TIME?"

©2013

Randy CFH.

<u>THE</u> WORST DATING LINES

130

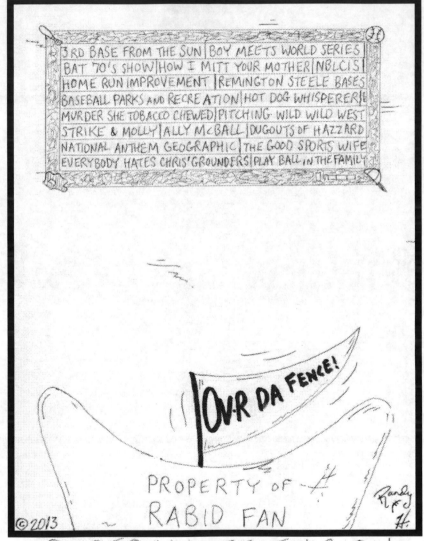

3RD BASE FROM THE SUN | BOY MEETS WORLD SERIES
BAT 70's SHOW | HOW I MITT YOUR MOTHER | NBLCIS |
HOME RUN IMPROVEMENT | REMINGTON STEELE BASES
BASEBALL PARKS AND RECREATION | HOT DOG WHISPERER |
MURDER SHE TOBACCO CHEWED | PITCHING WILD WILD WEST
STRIKE & MOLLY | ALLY McBALL | DUGOUTS OF HAZZARD
NATIONAL ANTHEM GEOGRAPHIC | THE GOOD SPORTS WIFE
EVERYBODY HATES CHRIS' GROUNDERS | PLAY BALL IN THE FAMILY

OVR DA FENCE!

PROPERTY OF
RABID FAN

© 2013

BASEBALL TELEVISION

HOT YOGA

STARVING ARTISTS

UNKNOWN MOMENTS IN MUSIC HISTORY, PART 2

WHEN THE RICH AND POWERFUL
GO ATOP THE EMPIRE STATE BUILDING

The SEMI-SCARY ⬡ ? MOVIE HOUSE

now playing:

"ROSEMARY'S BABY FINGER"

coming soon:

"GUMS: THE DENTURE'S -REVENGE"   "MELLOW PSYCHO"

"THE SHINING SILVERWARE"

"A MILDLY DISTURBING DREAM ON ELM STREET"

"THE SINGING & DANCING EXORCIST"

"HECKRAISER"

"SATURDAY THE 14TH: JASON'S WEEKEND"

"CUJO GETS FIXED"

"NOWHERE NEAR A FATAL ATTRACTION"

"THE HILLS HAVE CROSSED EYES"

"POLTERGEIST: THE BORING, NON-SUPERNATURAL DAY AFTER"

©2013

NOT-SO-FRIGHTENING HORROR FILMS

THE SCI-FI CHANNEL MOVIE "BENJI ON THE PLANET OF GIANT CATS"

141

STAND-UP COMEDY SANTA WORKS THE TOY ROOM

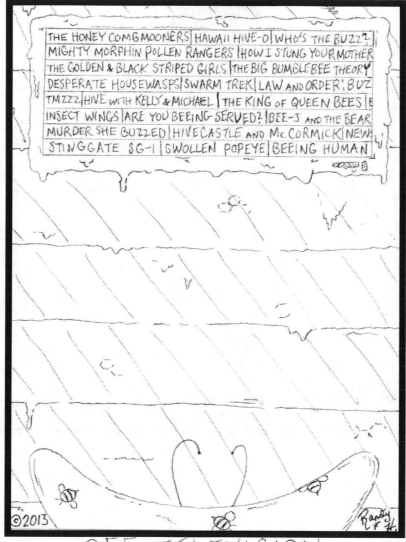

BEE TELEVISION

144

ACTOR ADRIEN BRODY GOES CAMPING

THE VERY FIRST THANKSGIVING: A FORESHADOWING OF FUTURE GATHERINGS

OYSTER BLIND DATES

Expectant ⚥ cinema

Randy *H ©2013

— now playing:
"NINE MONTHS SHOWING"

coming soon:

"THE BIRTHING OF A NATION"
"LABOR PAIN & GAIN"
"SHOW BLOAT"
"ABOUT A BOY OR A GIRL"
"THE MATRIX EXPECTING"
"MATERNITY DRESSED TO KILL"
"BIG NERVOUS DADDY"
"THANK YOU FOR SMOKING CIGARS"
"CONTRACTION THE BARBARIAN"
"MIGHTY MORPHINE POWER RANGERS: THE MOVIE"
"A WAITING ROOM WITH A VIEW"
"MA & PA KETTLE POP ANOTHER OUT"
"THE ULTRASOUND OF MUSIC"
"FEELING MINNESOTA'S TUMMY"
"CRAZY STUPID LOVE OF FOOD CRAVINGS"

PREGNANT PICTURES

FRESHMEN AT WORK
JOHN MELLENCAMPUS
KEGGER CHESNEY
CROWDED FRAT HOUSE
SOPHOMORE B. HAWKINS
JOHNNY HAZES JAZZ
BURNING MIDNIGHT OIL FOR EXAMS
THREE DORMS DOWN
STRICT DEAN MARTIN
CO-EDDIE MONEY
PRINCE OF PARTYING
MICHAEL PENNANT
NOTORIOUS B.M.O.C.
THE HUMAN IVY LEAGUE
NO DOUBT MY BRAIN IS FRIED

COLLEGE JUKEBOXES

THE ALTERNATE OPENING TO T.V.'s "BONANZA"

151

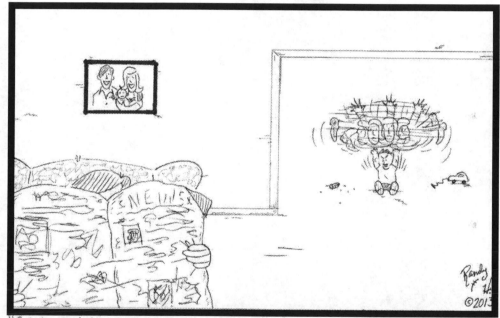

"SAY, HONEY--HOW ARE THOSE NEW PERFORMANCE ENHANCEMENT KIDS' CHEWABLES WORKING OUT FOR LITTLE TIMMY!... UM, HONEY?..."

BARNYARD BROADWAY, PART 2

154

"DON'T ASK."

ALTERED **Mouse** MOVIE HOUSE

now playing:

Randy # H. © 2013

"AMERICAN BEAUTY AND THE BEAST"

coming soon:

"ALADDIN ABOUT EVE"
"THE LION KING IN WINTER"
"TOY SOLDIERS STORY"
"THE HUNCHBACK OF NOTRE AUNTIE MAME"
"HER-CULES ALIBI"
"HOUSE ON POCA-HAUNTED HILL"
"MULAN ROUGE"
"A BUG'S LIFE IS BEAUTIFUL"
"AS GOOD AS IT GETS FOR TARZAN"
"HOW STELLA GOT HER EMPEROR'S NEW
GROOVE BACK"
"ATLANTIS: THE LOST EMPIRE STRIKES
BACK"
"MONEYBALL MONSTERS, INC."
"NEVER SAY FINDING NEMO AGAIN"

OTHER FILMS, DISNEY-STYLE: PART 2

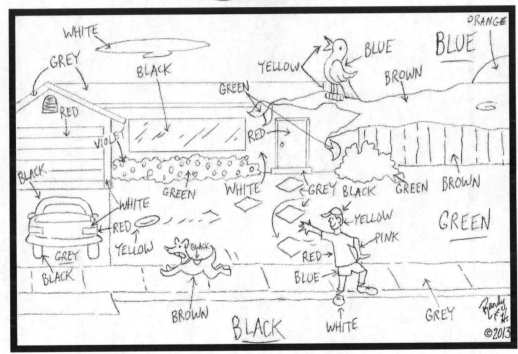

IF LIFE HAD CHEAP, TACKY COLORIZATION

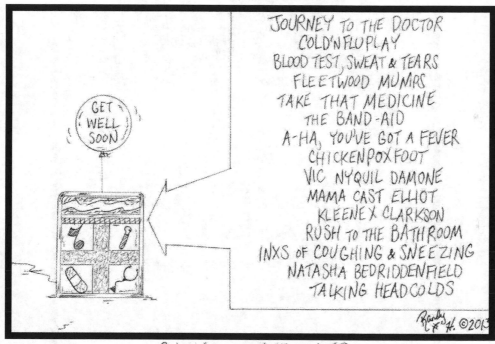

SICK JUKEBOXES

BREAKFAST TELEVISION

159

THE ONE-EYED, ONE-HORNED FLYING PURPLE PEOPLE EATER

IT WAS A FUN RIDE WHILE IT LASTED. JUST A CUTE LITTLE NOVELTY SONG THAT MADE IT BIG BACK THEN. AND I SUCKED THE FAME AND FORTUNE DRY LIKE A MILKSHAKE! I PARTIED HARD. I LOST MOST OF MY MONEY. BUT HARD TO FORGET A GUY LIKE ME! FOLKS REMEMBER I'VE SURVIVED DOING NOSTALGIA GIGS. NOTHING PERSONAL, BUT IF I HEAR ONE MORE TWERP SINGING THAT SONG ON THE STREET... I REALLY AM GONNA EAT 'EM!!

THE VH1 SERIES "BEHIND THE MUSIC: MONSTERS COPING WITH SUCCESS"

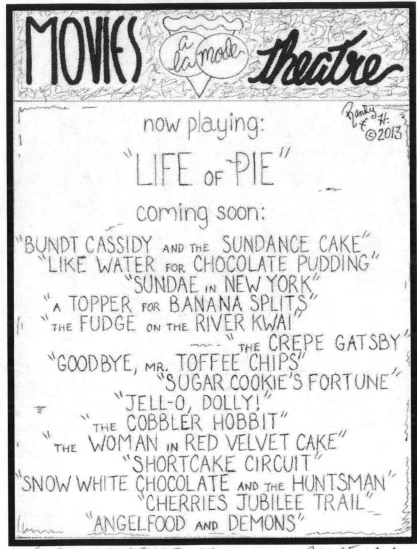

MOVIES a la mode theatre

Randy H. ©2013

now playing:
"LIFE of PIE"

coming soon:
"BUNDT CASSIDY AND THE SUNDANCE CAKE"
"LIKE WATER FOR CHOCOLATE PUDDING"
"SUNDAE IN NEW YORK"
"A TOPPER FOR BANANA SPLITS"
"THE FUDGE ON THE RIVER KWAI"
"THE CREPE GATSBY"
"GOODBYE, MR. TOFFEE CHIPS"
"SUGAR COOKIE'S FORTUNE"
"JELL-O, DOLLY!"
"THE COBBLER HOBBIT"
"THE WOMAN IN RED VELVET CAKE"
"SHORTCAKE CIRCUIT"
"SNOW WHITE CHOCOLATE AND THE HUNTSMAN"
"CHERRIES JUBILEE TRAIL"
"ANGELFOOD AND DEMONS"

JUST DESSERTS AT THE CINEMA

WHY WAS SVEN CONSIDERED THE BEST MASSAGE THERAPIST IN TOWN? PERHAPS IT WAS HIS "DETACHED" STYLE AND WONDROUS "MAGIC FINGERS" THAT DID THE TRICK...

FROTHY PROGRESSIONS

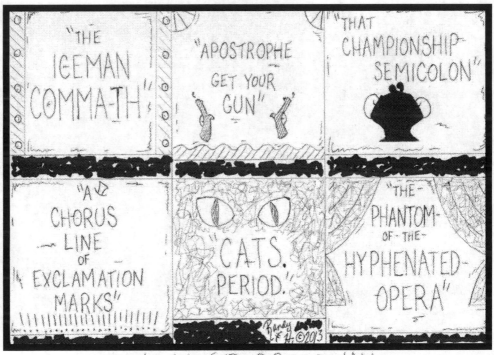

PUNCTUATED BROADWAY

165

VANCOUVER MORRISON
CONNIE FRANCE
GERMANY JACKSON
THE TOKYO POLICE
U.S.S.R. KELLY
AL GREENLAND
POLAND McCARTNEY
U.K.D. LANG
VANILLA ICELAND
NEW DELHI KIDS ON THE BLOCK
BRAZIL PAISLEY
SYDNEY VICIOUS
TIJUANA TURNER
ALDO NOVA SCOTIA
THE MAUI MOTELS

GLOBETROTTING JUKEBOXES

A CAUTIONARY VERSION OF AN OLD JOKE

SHOOTING THE CONSTRUCTION BREEZE

GRIM REALITY IN TOY CONCEPTS: "THE TAXMAN SAYS" SEE 'N SAY

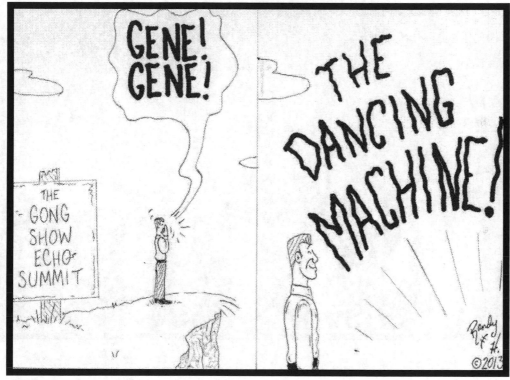

DR. THICKHEAD, THE MOST CLUELESS JAMES BOND VILLAIN, PART 5

SPORTS JUKEBOXES, PART 2

BALLOON GYMS

T.V.'s "CLOWN LOVE CONNECTION"

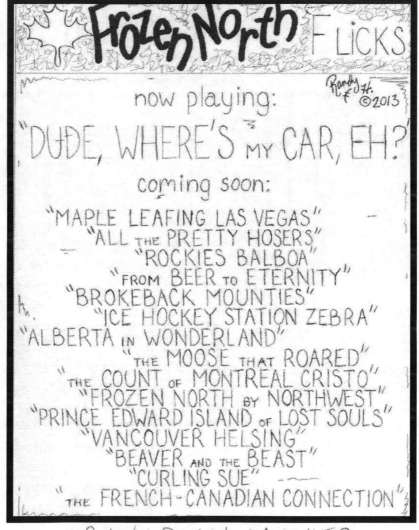

Frozen North FLICKS

now playing:
Randy F H. ©2013

"DUDE, WHERE'S MY CAR, EH?"

coming soon:

"MAPLE LEAFING LAS VEGAS"
"ALL THE PRETTY HOSERS"
"ROCKIES BALBOA"
"FROM BEER TO ETERNITY"
"BROKEBACK MOUNTIES"
"ICE HOCKEY STATION ZEBRA"
"ALBERTA IN WONDERLAND"
"THE MOOSE THAT ROARED"
"THE COUNT OF MONTREAL CRISTO"
"FROZEN NORTH BY NORTHWEST"
"PRINCE EDWARD ISLAND OF LOST SOULS"
"VANCOUVER HELSING"
"BEAVER AND THE BEAST"
"CURLING SUE"
"THE FRENCH-CANADIAN CONNECTION"

CANADIAN MOVIES

O.C.D. RESTROOMS

THE NEW BATMAN VILLAIN "THE GOOGLER"

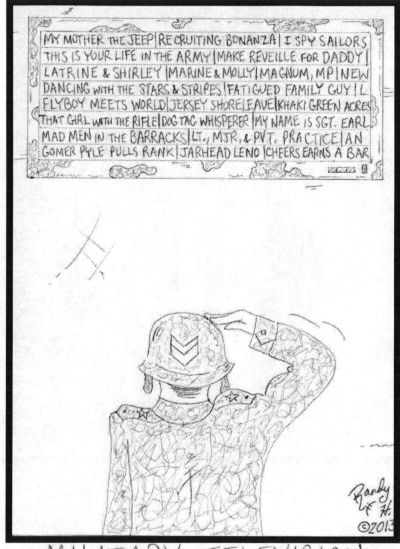

MY MOTHER THE JEEP | RECRUITING BONANZA | I SPY SAILORS | THIS IS YOUR LIFE IN THE ARMY | MAKE REVEILLE FOR DADDY | LATRINE & SHIRLEY | MARINE & MOLLY | MAGNUM, MP | NEW DANCING WITH THE STARS & STRIPES | FATIGUED FAMILY GUY | L FLYBOY MEETS WORLD | JERSEY SHORE LEAVE | KHAKI GREEN ACRES THAT GIRL WITH THE RIFLE | DOG TAG WHISPERER | MY NAME IS SGT. EARL MAD MEN IN THE BARRACKS | LT., MJR., & PVT. PRACTICE | AN GOMER PYLE PULLS RANK | JARHEAD LENO | CHEERS EARNS A BAR

MILITARY TELEVISION

THREE HOUND DOG NIGHT
THE GRASS ROOSTERS
BLUE OYSTER COW
OINK-O BOINGO
BAAA-HA MEN
DON HEN-LEY
RACCOON TRAVIS
PINK POSSUM
MULES WITHOUT HATS
BAY CRITTER ROLLERS
CHICAGO BEARS
SHERYL BLACK CROW
KID BILLY GOAT ROCK
RATT-LERS
CAT-PHISH

COUNTRY CRITTER JUKEBOXES

DISNEY'S "FLATFACE FELIX: THE CAT THAT CAN'T LAND ON HIS FEET"

TECH SUPPORT	ONLINE SURVEYS
HELP: JUST CLICK YOUR MOUSE. CUSTOMER: OK. BUT IT'LL TAKE A WHILE. I HAVE TO CATCH ONE FIRST.	Q: WOULD YOU LIKE TO TAKE OUR SURVEY? A: NO THANKS. I DON'T DO DRUGS.
DATING SERVICES	DUNCE FACEBOOK
SINGLES.COM: WE FOUND THE PERFECT MATCH FOR YOU! MEMBER: BUT I WANTED A WOMAN!	THIS IDIOT WOULD LIKE TO BE YOUR FRIEND. (CONFIRM) (IGNORE-AMUS)

INTERNET FOR MORONS

DOUBLE MEDIA theater

now playing:

"GET SMART, FORREST GUMP"

coming soon:

"GONE WITH THE WINDS OF WAR"
"MY FAVORITE MARTIAN BRUNETTE"
"HARRY POTTER AND THE GOBLET OF FIREFLY"
"THERE'S SOMETHING ABOUT MARY TYLER MOORE"
"BEVERLY HILLS COP, 90210"
"TWO AND A HALF MEN IN BLACK"
"THE BIG LEBOWSKI BANG THEORY"
"THE LOVE BUG M*A*S*H ED"
"...AND JUSTICE FOR ALL IN THE FAMILY"
"THE GODFATHER KNOWS BEST"
"TEEN AIRWOLF"
"WHAT ABOUT BOB NEWHART?"
"STAR TREK WARS"
"TRUE BLOOD GRIT"
"GOODBYE, COLUMBO"

Randy F. H.
©2013

THE SMALL SCREEN INVADES THE BIG SCREEN
(OR VICE VERSA)

184

CONTENTS

1

EDITH BUNKER'S DINGBAT CASSEROLE

Randy H. ©2013

~ ONE HEAPING CUP OF CONTROVERSY
~ SEASON WITH BIGOTRY
~ STIR IN BOWL GENEROUSLY
~ POUR MIXTURE IN CASSEROLE BAKING DISH
~ SPRINKLE LITTLE GOIL ON TOP
~ BEFORE BAKING, HAVE MEATHEAD TASTE FOR FLAVOR
~ PUT IN OVEN AT 400°, AND BAKE 45 MINS. MEANWHILE, STIFLE YOURSELF AND SIT ON TUR-LET UNTIL DONE.

(THIS RECIPE WAS TAPED BEFORE A LIVE STUDIO AUDIENCE)

THE NORMAN LEAR RECIPE COOKBOOK

184

185

185

THE TRANSVESTITE SAFARI SERIES "DRAG COUNTRY"

ELVIS PRESLEY COSTELLO
ROY CLARK ORBISON
JOHN LENNON MAYER
GRATEFUL DEAD OR ALIVE
JACKSON MAROON 5
PEARL JAM BAILEY
BOY GEORGE HARRISON
OLIVIA NEWTON-JOHN DENVER
MOTLEY CUTTING CRUE
RICKY DEAN MARTIN
R.E.M. KELLY
BEASTIE BACKSTREET BOYS
SLY AND THE FAMILY ROLLING STONES
COLLECTIVE SOUL ASYLUM
JUSTIN TIMBERLAKE BIEBER

MIXED-UP JUKEBOXES

MONSTER BROADWAY

SPOILED, WHINING BIRDS OF PREY

BAD IDEA GUESSING GAMESHOWS

another

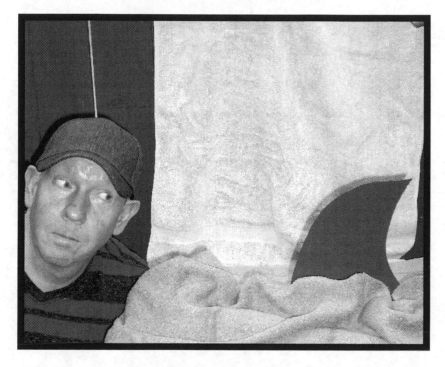

The critics approacheth...

In spite of unpredictable weather,
it was fun (as usual) posing with
the shark fin while my niece/photographer
Shelby Rose Foster clicked away.
Thanks for the fifth go-round, Bugs!

look for these other
LEFT FIELD titles...
™

Which Way to Left Field?
Left Field, Reloaded
Left Field Strikes Back!
Left Field Controls the Universe
Left Field...in Glorious Toonarama

www.createspace.com
www.authorhouse.com
www.amazon.com

- - - - - - -

(uncensored)

Left Field Raw
Left Field Raw, Vol. 2
Left Field Raw, Vol. 3

www.48hrbooks.com

Printed in the United States
By Bookmasters